REDO YOUR ROOM

50 BEDROOM DIYS YOU CAN DO IN A WEEKEND

Produced by Jessica D'Argenio Waller

ZONDERKIDZ

Redo Your Room
Copyright © 2015 Red Engine, LLC

Requests for information should be addressed to:
Zonderkidz, 3900 *Sparks Drive SE, Grand Rapids, Michigan 49546*

ISBN 978-0-310-74632-4

Done in association with Red Engine, LLC, Baltimore, MD

Zonderkidz is a trademark of Zondervan.

Writer and stylist: Jessica D'Argenio Waller
Editors: Jacque Alberta and Karen Bokram
Contributor: Katie Abbondanza
Cover and interior design: Chun Kim
Cover photography: Sean Scheidt

Printed in China

14 15 16 17 18 19 20 21 22 23 /DSC/ 10 9 8 7 6 5 4 3 2 1

CONTENTS

The room in your house where you spend the most time? It's probably your bedroom. With all that sleeping, hanging out, getting dressed and studying, it's amazing you ever leave!

And since that space is entirely yours, it should be a reflection of who you are. Maybe you're ready for a grown-up room, but don't want to give up all your favorite stuffed animals just yet. Use this book as a guide to transform your bedroom into a cute, comfortable, relaxing, inspiring and happy place--with space for all your memories.

Think that takes lots of time and lots of bucks? Nope. Inside are dozens of affordable, stylish crafts you can do yourself, like a floating ribbon chandelier or a postcard-covered nightstand— little touches that can instantly transform a boring bedroom into a space that's fun, fresh and feels totally you.

From your workspace to your closet, your walls to your windows, here are 50 chic crafts and cinchy DIYs to decorate your room. Try one this weekend!

—the editors

PERFECT PAINTING TIPS

We've got four secrets to scoring a perfect paint job. What happens if you mess up or decide baby blue isn't for you? Don't fret: it's just paint! Invest in a new can, and get an instant do-over.

1 **Mark it off.** Use painter's tape to tape off the floorboards, trim and any other areas that shouldn't be painted in your main wall color. Press firmly on the tape to ensure a good seal. Ask Mom or Dad to help you remove any outlet or light switch covers.

2 **Protect your stuff.** Lay a dropcloth or tarp over the floor in the area where you'll be painting in order to catch any drips. Wear old clothes and shoes that can get messy, too.

3 **Break out the brushes.** Open the paint can and give it a good stir with a wooden paint stick. Then, pour a small amount into a painting tray and affix a foam roller to the paint roller handle. Roll the foam roller in the paint a few times until it's fully coated, then apply paint to the wall.

4 **Get rollin'.** Paint in a W motion, going up and down at angles to ensure the best coverage. Once the wall is covered, move on to another wall while one dries. Wait at least 24 hours before applying a second coat of paint.

{ 10 STEPS TO REDOING YOUR ROOM }

**Here's the full process from start to finish.
Wanna skip a step? Go for it!**

1. Ask your parents (OK, no skipping this step!)
2. Stash your kiddie stuff
3. Make a vision journal to hone your inspo
4. Focus on your room's zones and sketch your rearranging ideas
5. Choose the perfect paint color
6. Paint, then move the furniture into place
7. Start organizing and cut the clutter
8. Get smart about storage
9. Make it lovely with flowers, window treatments and lighting
10. Create cute crafts

RED Primary red is a very active and energizing color. It's a vibrant hue that will get your blood flowing—maybe not a perfect choice if you like your room to keep you feeling calm and centered.

ORANGE Another vivid color, orange is totally stimulating (great for workouts) but can be a little too loud for a bedroom. A muted amber hue might feel just right, however.

YELLOW Yellow is sunny, and keeps you happy. Try a few different swatches of the sunshine shade to make sure you get the exact color you want—without veering into school bus territory.

GREEN Green is both warm and inviting, and can create a peaceful space. When paired with white furniture, any shade of green will really stand out.

BLUE The most productive color, soft shades of blue also add a grounding, calming presence. If you tend to study mostly in your room, consider this cool hue.

PINK A bold pink adds a warm and exciting element to any space. It's fun and fresh and a pure pop of color that can be unexpected. Mute it with white accessories and bring in other shades of pink for a super pretty room.

PURPLE Light purple is a passive color that can have a great de-stressing effect, while dark purple feels lush and elegant. Pale purples also pair gorgeously with navy blue and crisp white. Ahhh....

WHITE White walls can be peaceful, but also can look stark if the room isn't decorated just right. A good way to avoid the bare minimalist look is to repeat the white throughout other pieces in your room: a white duvet, dresser or chair can echo the calm, clean feeling of ivory paint.

Study: Your homework nook should have a sturdy desk, a bright work lamp and a comfy (but not too cozy!) chair.

Fun: Leave some open space on the floor, slide a chair beneath a window or pile up some pillows in the corner, then add a stack of books, magazines and your headphones for blissing out.

Before you actually get to the heavy lifting, break out the pencil and paper (and, if necessary, tape measure). Sketch out where you think your furniture should go, drawing items to approximate scale. Get your draft approved by Mom and Dad, then ask for their assistance with the moving. With a plan in mind, it'll be easier to get everything into the right place.

{ 3 RULES FOR REARRANGING }

1. BED GOES FIRST: Deciding the placement of your bed is step one—it's the biggest piece of the puzzle, and it will set the groundwork for the rest of the furniture. Test out a few options to make sure you like where you're going to be sleeping.

2. FIND THE FLOW: Push your bed and desk against a wall, and then balance with other big furniture, like a bookcase or dresser. Make sure the flow makes sense: you don't want to have to climb over a chair to get to your closet each day.

3. WIDE-OPEN WINDOWS: Turn a window into a focal point by placing a desk or comfy reading chair underneath it. Got a small room? Hang a mirror on the wall perpendicular to a window to bounce in more light. It works!

CHOOSING THE RIGHT HUE

Picking paint colors is one of the most fun parts of redecorating. Maybe you love that bright pink found in the pattern of your duvet cover. Maybe you want to match the pale purple lilac flowers you love in Mom's garden. Or perhaps you're beginning with a blank slate and need a little direction. That's where we come in!

The colors you choose can influence your mood more than you might think. From riotous red to blissful blue, flip the page to learn the secret effect of hues...

PLAN YOUR VISION

Before you delve too deeply into the world of design, (hello, Pinterest overload!) begin thinking about how you want your new room to look. Pink and girly? Calm and cool? Vintage and bright?

Here's a good way to decide what's truly y-o-u: start a vision journal. Grab a notebook, scissors and a stack of magazines. Start clipping out images that inspire you. Make lists of ideas you want your dream room to incorporate. Use a glue stick to paste your inspiration photos into your notebook, then pencil in any notes, edits or changes along the way.

While flipping through your vision journal, your subconscious design sense will start to show through—and help make the room redecorating process much more cohesive and thematic.

Maybe you're drawn to flowers over stripes, hearts over stars or magenta over turquoise. Making these small decisions now will give you a clearer idea later when choosing themes for your DIY crafts, picking the perfect wall paint and even all the way down to selecting the tiny trinkets coming into your new space.

{ STASH IT }

Smart secrets for storing your kiddie stuff:

STUFFED ANIMALS: Use big baskets to house your fluffy friends.
PICTURE BOOKS: Save your faves, donate the rest to your library.
TOYS AND TRINKETS: That collection of snow globes you've had since you were four? Keep a select few and place them around your room for a layered look. Donate the rest or store for safekeeping.

UTILIZE YOUR SPACE

Your room is your haven: it's where you sleep, where you study and where you have fun, so it might be a good idea to divide your four walls into these three zones to easily designate each area.

Zone It Out
Break it down: Your room master plan

Sleep: Position your bed, nightstand, reading lamp, as well as a bench for storage if there's room. Leave space for kneeling bedside to say your nightly prayers.

CHAPTER ONE

SHAPE YOUR SPACE

Redoing a room shouldn't be a strict or serious undertaking. Have fun…and make it all yours!

MOVIN' ON UP

For the last few years, you've been spending your allowance on shoes instead of stuffed animals. Chapter books? Swapped for textbooks. Cartoons? Try hilarious YouTube vids. If this sounds like you, it's time to rework your room into a place that suits who you are now.

The first step to transforming your space is getting your parents' approval on the project. Schedule a time to have a chat about revamping your bedroom. (Here's a hint: do it when they're not busy or distracted.)

Things to Tackle

Talking about transitioning your room can be a big discussion. Make a list of main points so you can cover everything in one go.

Out with the old: Show your parents you can take responsibility for the change. Set a date to sort through your stuff and decide what you'll keep, what you'll donate to church or a charity and what you'll toss out. (More on this in chapter 2!)

Find a theme: Maybe ballet was your thing in second grade, but now it's Paris. Ask your parents if you can swap your pointe-shoe-pink paint for something a little more chic, like black-and-white stripes on one wall or a gallery of French postcards.

Keeping the keepsakes: You don't have to erase all remnants of your elementary school days (hey, those early years made you the amazing girl you are today!). Decide what projects and papers you want to hang on to and display them in a binder or memory box.

One thing to remember: Make sure your room stays a reflection of who you were *then* as much as who you are now. This isn't about tossing once-treasured toys to make space for newer stuff. Keep a few favorites neatly displayed in baskets and bookcases.

CHAPTER TWO

GET
ORGANIZED

**Everything from bedtime routines to weekend rituals are
made easier when your stuff is in the right place.**

MAKE A PLAN

Whether you're a clutter queen or a neatnik, we bet ya understand
the benefits of knowing where your stuff is...at least most of the
time. Now that your room is rearranged, it's time to figure out where
your most treasured belongings will fit into your master plan.

With our space-saving tips, clutter-battling tricks and quick
categorizing techniques, it'll be a cinch to keep your room tidy. But
making your bed every day? That's all you!

Cut the clutter

Sorting through your stuff can be a pretty major process. The key
is to start small. Begin in one area of your room (your desk, for
example), and create three piles: keep, toss and donate.

Your beloved pencil case from third grade? If you haven't
used it in more than a year, it's time to let it go. We know it's tough:
the things we keep tend to be associated with strong memories,
and it's difficult to separate the nostalgia from the item itself.

Our tip? Photograph any object you used to love but don't use
anymore, then pass it on to another girl who may treasure it, too.
Donate clothing, books or toys to a church rummage sale or send
them to a disaster relief program to help someone truly in need.

Bottom line? If it's not pretty, meaningful or useful, donate it.
On the other hand, you can always rework your fave old things into
totally new uses. Get crafty!

Rework it, girl

Transform your childhood faves into cute new stuff.

Camp tees: Turn 'em into cozy pillows with our how-to on page 43.

Fave photos: Scan pics to make a photo calendar or incorporate
them into our snapshot photo garland on page 58.

Old tests and essays: Show off a couple faves on a clipboard pin wall (page 29) or store a few from each grade in a big binder you can add to in the years to come.

Postcards: Make a cool collage on your wall or behind your door, or create a postcard nightstand (check out page 46).

SAVE SPACE

Now that you know exactly what you have, it's time to stash it. While seeing all your options is sometimes a good thing (like with your shoes), at other times viewing every last one of your possessions can be visually overwhelming.

Here's an insider secret: Clean and bare surfaces create the feeling of a neat and tidy room. So pick just two or three specimens from your seashell collection and store the rest in a safe place. You can always swap them out for different shells next month.

As far as your closet, change it with the seasons. You won't need your winter sweaters in the middle of July, so at the start of summer, store them, clean and neatly folded, in a soft case under your bed. Same goes with shorts, bathing suits and sandals at the beginning of fall. The clothes and shoes you *do* leave in your closet will have much more room to breathe, and you'll be able to focus on what you've got, which means more creative outfits!

Store it smart
Here's where to stash your stuff.

Shoes: An over-the-door shoe rack is stellar for keeping all your pairs together. Store fancy, less-worn shoes in their original boxes on a shelf, where they won't collect dust.

Sweaters: Keep them neatly folded in a drawer, arranged by weight: heaviest on the bottom.

Jeans: Roll each pair and line up the rolls in a drawer.

Skirts: Go to a home store and snag a hanger with multiple tiers and use it to hang skirts of all lengths without sacrificing space.

T-shirts: Fold them neatly and stack tall. Then turn the whole stack on its side and place in a drawer. It's like a library for tees!

Magazines: Stash your faves in magazine holders (find at IKEA) and store on a shelf. Label with the name and year for easy finding.

Books: Books are best stored on a shelf—make yours more fun with our floating wall shelves on page 72.

Trinkets and treasures: Shadow boxes are great for curating small displays; sturdy storage boxes are perfect for preserving heirlooms you'd like to keep for years to come but don't need to look at daily.

CATEGORIZE CLEVERLY

Here's the big challenge: Remembering where you stored all that stuff. Our best tip? Label everything. Whether you have a fancy label maker or just use masking tape and a Sharpie, writing a quick list of contents helps you find the items you need—fast.

When packing things up to store in the basement, make sure to mark boxes with your name and what's inside, like picture books, dolls or toys. That way, you'll know what's where if you need it.

And if your closet is still crammed full? Draw a map for the door. Noting exactly where your winter boots are will help you locate them before the snow melts.

Desk details

Is your desk buried under a sea of papers, pens and pencils? Take back your workspace with handy organizers for all that clutter. Chalkboard-painted mason jars (page 26) can corral small items you use frequently.

Make your desk drawers a cheery place for notepads, calculators and other tools with our decoupage tips on page 20. Stock up on fun-patterned file organizers for tests and essays from the current school year that you might need to reference, and keep a recycling bin under your desk for papers you no longer need.

Closet clues

We've spent years perfecting our closet organizing technique. Start by arranging similar items together (shirts with shirts, etc.), and then color-coordinate each section. It sounds a little wacky, but it creates a cute, boutique-like system, which lets you know where everything is at a glance.

And because closets can go from organized to disaster in seconds, take 15 minutes each week to rearrange your threads (hint: do it as you stash your clean laundry). For extra credit, hang clothes on the same type of hanger and face them in the same direction to turn your humble closet into a gorgeous space.

CHAPTER THREE

SCULPT YOUR STYLE

Be selective when choosing the things that fill your room. Are they useful? Pretty? Or both? Both is best.

MAKING IT LOVELY

What turns any room into a space where you want to sit and stay awhile? Nice lighting, breezy windows and pretty extras like lush flowers or photos of your friends. Set your sights on those three elements to make your bedroom your insta-happy place.

Since your bed is the focal point of your room, spend some time making it look nice and feel super comfy. We're not saying you have to make your bed each morning—though your parents would probably appreciate it!—but a nicely styled bed creates a room that much more warm and inviting.

Make things easy by picking out a coordinating comforter or duvet and a couple pillow shams. One or two throw pillows add a stylish touch. Keeping your nightstand neat and tidy helps, too.

Bedroom dos and don'ts

DO Wake up to something pretty. A bud vase with a bloom, a poster you love or a quote illustrated on your wall will make skipping the snooze button way easier.

DON'T Try not to push your bed into the corner, leaving no room to actually get in it. Space on either side makes it easier to make it as well.

DO Show off your treasured teddy, but a pile of stuffed animals of all shapes and sizes makes actual sleeping crowded—and your bed overly cluttered.

DON'T Forget to have a super cozy blanket folded neatly at the foot of your bed—perfect for quick after-school naps (no need to get under the sheets!) or for adding a bright burst of complementary color and texture. Use it to cuddle up with while studying at your desk, too.

Let in the light

Whether you're reading in bed, working at your desk or winding down after a busy day, the lighting you use makes a difference in how you feel. Choosing the right light makes your room that much more comfortable and functional.

GLOW GIRL
Here are the three lamps your room should have:

Night light: Low wattage for getting ready for bed. Try a small lamp on your nightstand, or a pretty night light that plugs into the wall for a soft glow once you're asleep.

Reading lamp: A small, bright lamp is ideal to clip onto your headboard (or even on the back cover of your book) for reading a few pages before you fall asleep.

Desk lamp: A good light with a flexible stand is key to keeping you alert and your eyes in focus—especially on all those algebra equations and vocab words.

Don't forget the sun! Throwing open the windows lets in a fresh burst of breeze while bringing in natural light. Stick with a pair of sheer curtains to open during the day and a good set of blinds that you can close at night. Tiny plants (try succulents) on your windowsill do wonders for making your space feel alive and lived-in—and they don't require much attention.

A HAPPY PLACE

Seeing a whole wall full of things that inspire you every time you walk into your room is the best recipe for transforming a space into your personal haven.

Stake out a spot above your bed, desk or even behind your door for a collage of things that encourage creativity, faith and positivity. Print out your favorite Bible quotes, clip photos from magazines, borrow pictures from family photo albums and/or print out a few inspiring travel shots from around the web.

Use this wall as a vision board for current achievements, future goals and distant dreams—and don't be afraid to change it up.

Gettin' cozy

Cushy comforters, plush pillows and beyond-soft blankets can make a cold four-walled room into a relaxing nook. Here are some secrets to bringing in new textures to transform your space.

MIXED MEDIA
Make room for these four elements:

String lights: Strung around a window, door or bedframe, twinkly white lights do wonders for ambience. The more, the merrier!

Fuzzy textures: Faux sheepskin throws and furry pillows add a chic lushness to your bed, desk chair or window seat, Try mixing in a range of hues and textures for a totally glam-yet-cozy style.

Metallic lamps: Whether you go gold or silver, make sure your metals match. A gold lamp on your nightstand should ideally coordinate with the light on your desk for a cohesive look.

Mirrors: It's true what they say: mirrors make any room look bigger, but they also serve a purpose. Go for three: A floor-length one on the wall for eyeing outfits, a higher one for atop your dresser to check jewelry placement and a smaller handheld mirror for getting a view of the back of your hair.

Where you work

Do you find that inspiration strikes best when you're studying at your desk, the kitchen table or on the floor? We're working out what work (be that school stuff or me-time) is best done where.

Your bed: Doing homework in bed sure can be comfy, but it can also lead to problems falling asleep when you're ready to hit the pillow. Using your bed for studying and schoolwork isn't what it's meant for—and you can confuse your brain as far as what should be happening when. Reading for fun, however, is a whole other story. The verdict: Keep the textbooks off the bed.

In front of the TV: Curled up on the couch with a book sounds more like a recipe for relaxation than studying. Relegate the couch to hanging out and make it a no-homework zone so you'll have more fun when you do have time to lounge around.

Your desk: Sitting upright in a desk chair with a bendy lamp is the easiest place to focus. It's free from distractions, encourages good posture (which helps you think better!) and gives you the privacy and quiet you need to focus. Just make sure your desk doesn't get covered in papers: having room to work is half the battle.

Anywhere but your room: Taking over the dining room table might be a hindrance when dinner is served, but it's a good place to spread out and center all your supplies in one (temporary) space. Having literal room to think can help free your brain of unnecessary clutter, too. Ahhh....

SMARTEN UP YOUR STUDY SPACE

Every girl needs an inspired study space: A place to work that's cute and clutter-free. If your desk is messy and you've misplaced every last pen and pencil, hunkering down to do homework is even more of a chore. From crafty inboxes to help you stay organized to an inspiring clipboard pin wall, here are eight brilliant ways to spruce up your desk.

✳ Crafty Fabric Book Covers

Leave brown paper bags behind and give your books a make-over with fun fabrics that'll surely stand out from the stack.

WHAT YOU'LL DO

1. On a flat surface, lay out fabric and place your textbook on top.

2. Open the book cover and use a ruler to mark a 3" border on the left and right sides of the book. Mark a 2" border on the top and bottom sides of the book. Cut out the fabric book cover.

3. On the top border, find where the book's spine will lay and cut out a small rectangle the width of the book's spine. Repeat on bottom.

4. Crease the horizontal side of the border over the front cover. It's helpful to lift up each cover when creasing to keep everything smooth. Use tape to hold fabric cover in place.

5. Tuck down the corners on the tall side as if you were wrapping a gift and secure in place with tape. Close the book and repeat steps 4 and 5 on the back cover. You totally get an "A" if you use fabrics that match with each subject.

Instant Update

Add your own signature to make a serious statement.

REMEMBER WHEN: Carry your memories of summer camp into fall by using the front of a tie-dyed tee as a book cover. Bonus points if it has autographs from your bunkmates.

DENIM DAZE: Cut off the legs of an old pair of jeans and use the back portion with pockets as your book cover. Bling out the pockets with iron-on studs.

SECRET STORAGE: After wrapping your book, arrange stretchy elastic headbands in an "X" pattern over the front cover. Then tuck in pencils, photos and notes.

✳ Decoupaged Desk Drawers

A quick collage on the bottoms of your drawers makes them so cute, you'll be searching for excuses to open them.

✗ QUICK 'N' EASY

WHAT YOU'LL DO

1. Cut out photos from magazines and lay them out on your drawer bottoms to see how they fit. Overlap them or position them in whatever way you like.

2. Use the paintbrush to coat the bottom of your desk drawer with a thin layer of Mod Podge. Then, coat the backs of your cutouts with Mod Podge, and press them in place on the drawer bottom.

3. Photos keep popping up? A little more Mod Podge should keep them in place.

4. Spread a thin layer of Mod Podge over the entire collage to make sure your project stays put.

5. Leave drawer open and let dry for a few hours before filling 'em with pencils, paper clips and notebooks.

TIP If your parents don't want you gluing your drawers directly, measure the inside and cut a piece of foam board (find it at the craft store) to fit inside your drawers. Decorate the board and slide it in for a stylish, commitment-free DIY.

WHAT YOU'LL NEED

- Magazines you love
- Foam paintbrush
- Mod Podge
- Scissors

✳ Chalkboard Pencil Jars

To corral clips and pins, coat Mason jars in chalkboard paint and label for easy access.

WHAT YOU'LL DO

1. Wash and dry the mason jar thoroughly.

2. Use the paintbrush to coat the jar with the paint. For the best results, let paint dry for 3 days before labeling the jar with the chalk.

3. Tie a piece of ribbon around the top of the jar and trim ends.

WHAT YOU'LL NEED
- Mason jar
- Chalkboard paint
- Foam paintbrush
- Chalk
- Ribbon
- Scissors

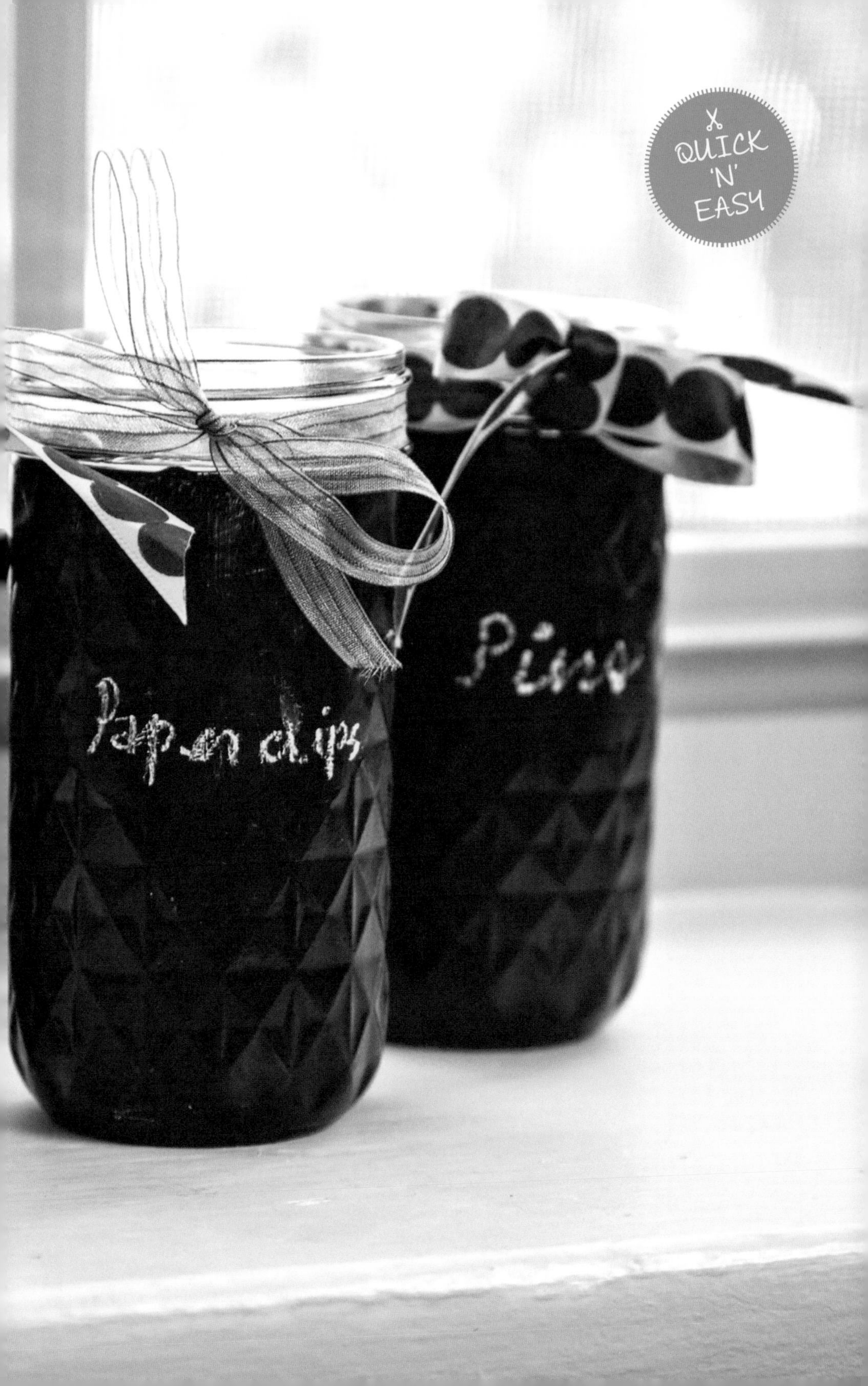
QUICK 'N' EASY
Paper clips
Pins

WHAT YOU'LL NEED

- Colorful Washi Tape
- 6 Clipboards
- Photos, postcards, magazine clippings or other images that inspire you
- 12 Adhesive-backed Velcro fasteners

✳ Clipboard Pin Wall

Use clipboards to flaunt colorful images that you can easily swap whenever you're in the mood for some fresh inspiration.

WHAT YOU'LL DO

1. Using the Washi tape, make fun designs or bright borders on each of the clipboards.

2. Affix 2 adhesives to the back of each clipboard. Map out your grid on the wall, then affix the other side of the adhesive strip to the wall and press clipboards into place.

3. Clip in your magazine pages and photos. Use more Washi tape if you need to layer.

4. Embellish your "pinboards" with friendship bracelets, cool earrings and bright bows.

✂ QUICK 'N' EASY

Or try it on mini chalkboards!

✳ Painted Wooden Desk Chair

Breathe new life into an old chair with a cheery, speedy paint job. Psst: Ask a parent for help.

WHAT YOU'LL DO

1. Wash the chair with a damp cloth to get rid of any dirt or cobwebs. Then let the chair air-dry completely.

2. Use sandpaper to sand the chair's surface to make it smooth and easy to paint.

3. Wipe the chair off with the cloth to remove any dust that accumulated from sanding.

4. Paint your chair with the color you chose and let it dry.

OPTIONAL A coat of high-gloss aerosol sealer will protect your sweet new seat.

Quickie Craft Alert!

3 fun ways to deck the walls above your desk.

FABRIC FLAGS: Scrap fabric cut into cute triangles and glued onto metallic cord looks darling pinned over your desk.

RIBBON BOWS: Tie tiny ribbon bows around a cord or twine for a girly garland to loop over the back of your chair.

METALLIC PAINT CHIPS: Stock up on metallic paint chips from the home supply store, then cut into circle shapes and punch holes in the top. String onto yarn and hang over your headboard for a shiny finish.

XXX
CRAFT QUEEN

27
AUGUST

WHAT YOU'LL NEED
- Wooden chair
- Cleaning rag
- Coarse grain sandpaper
- Satin-finish paint
- Paintbrush
- Aerosol sealant (optional)

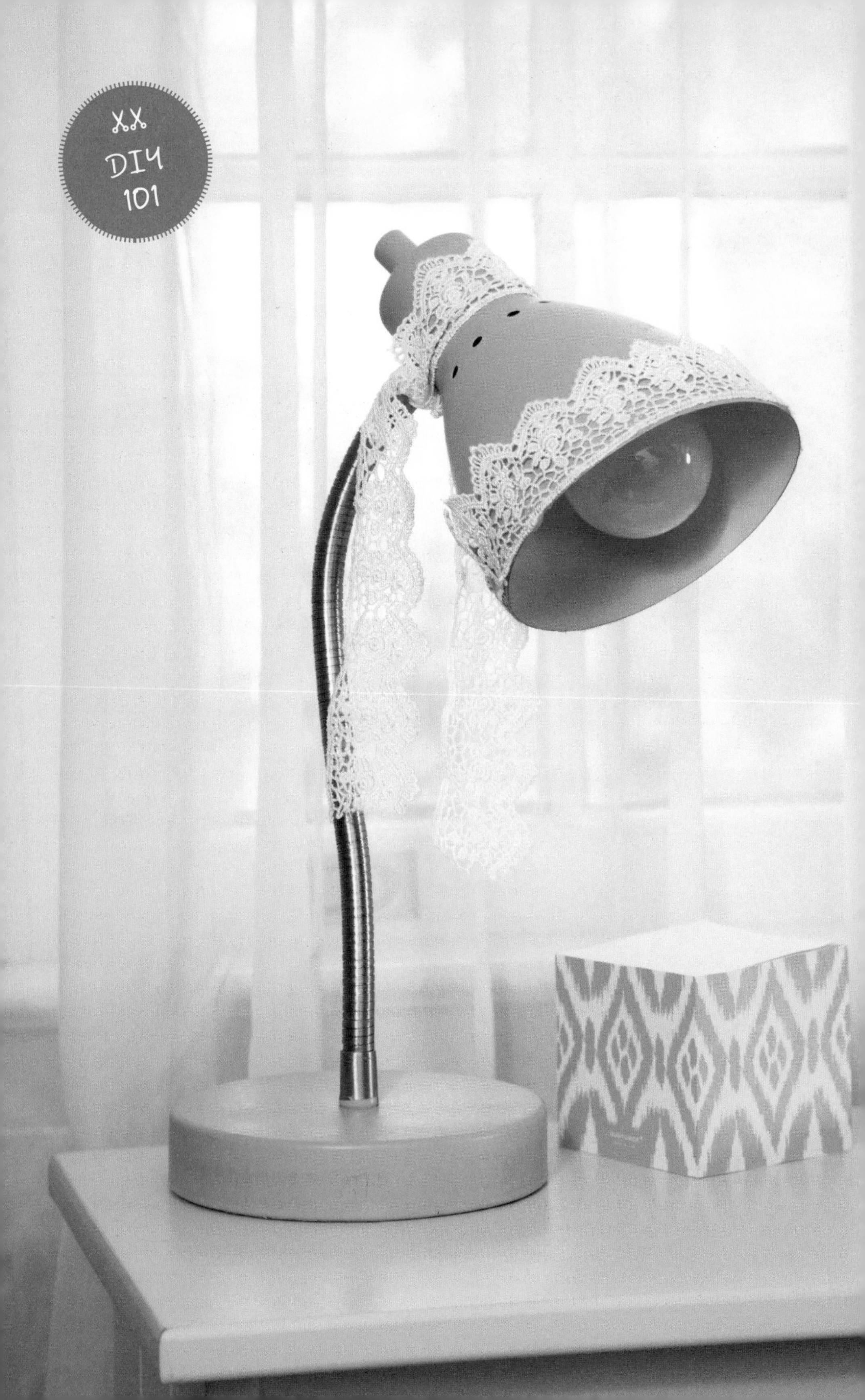
DIY
101

✳ Decorated Desk Lamp

A little lace and a coat of pretty paint add some extra shine to your standard homework light.

WHAT YOU'LL DO

1. Use painter's tape to protect the lamp pole and cord attachment so they remain paint-free.

2. Take the lamp outside and spray paint the surface of the shade and the base. Let dry at least one hour, and then remove the painter's tape.

3. Measure the lace trim around the opening of the lampshade and trim so edges just touch. Hot glue in place.

4. Measure the lace trim around the base of the lamp and trim so edges just touch, then hot glue in place.

WHAT YOU'LL NEED

- Metal desk lamp
- Painter's tape
- Spray paint in your favorite color
- Lace trim long enough to fit around diameter and base of lampshade
- Scissors
- Hot glue gun and some glue sticks

Free Fixes!

Got a lamp you want to revamp? Try our quick tricks for an easy (and free!) makeover...

JEWELED UP: Apply tiny jewels to the base and lampshade with a hot glue gun or craft glue for a glam-girl update.

BOWED OVER: A slew of ribbons tied in bows up the stem of the lamp is a chic touch.

ACCESSORIZE IT: Tie the stems of a few faux blooms around the shade. Mini flower crown!

Wild Washi Inbox

A basic letter holder might not look like much at the store, but a quick flick of Washi tape morphs it into a pretty place to stash your to-do lists, Post-It notes and planner.

WHAT YOU'LL NEED

- Letter organizer (wood, metal, cardboard or plastic is fine)
- Washi tape in a variety of colors and patterns
- Scissors

To do:
Walk spot
do dishes
make bed
read chapter 5

WHAT YOU'LL DO

1. Line up a strip of Washi tape along the top layer of one section in your inbox organizer, trimming to fit with scissors. Smooth out the tape so it lays in a straight, flat line.

2. Repeat with a different color or pattern of tape to make a design of your choosing. Try diagonal lines, vertical stripes or covering the entire organizer.

Quickie Craft Alert!

More easy DIY updates for any inbox:

PAINT JOB: Use neon nailpolish to add poppy polka dots to your letter holder.

DRAW SOMETHING: Get doodlin' with a black Sharpie to make cool line designs.

WRAP STAR: Bright wrapping paper can add a hit of pretty pattern in an instant.

✳ Cute Computer Cords

Dress up your dreary cords and you'll always be able to spot your wild wires from across the room.

WHAT YOU'LL DO

1. Decide on a Washi tape pattern for your power cord.

2. Cut a 1" piece of tape, then wrap it around the start of your cord. Repeat with the next color in your pattern, leaving a bit of space between each tape color.

3. Repeat for the length of your power cord, making sure all tape ends are pressed down firmly for a good seal.

WHAT YOU'LL NEED
- Power cord
- Washi tape in a variety of colors and patterns
- Scissors

DRESS UP YOUR BEDROOM

Your zen zone should be exactly that: a pretty place you can totally chill in. Your bed is the room's focal point, so fill it with plush pillows, a cool 'n' colorful headboard and sweet surroundings that help keep you calm and totally composed—but also look super cute.

✳ Cushy Fabric Headboard

Transform your old headboard into a completely you statement piece using a simple strip of fabric.

WHAT YOU'LL DO

1. Measure the width, height and depth of your headboard with the tape measure.

2. At the fabric store, head to the remnant section. Pick out a bolt large enough to cover the front of your headboard.

3. Use Duck Tape to hold the fabric in place over your headboard while you pull it taut, lining up the pattern of the fabric print if necessary.

4. With a parent's help, use a staple gun to attach the fabric to the back of your headboard.

OPTIONAL Make your headboard even more comfy by placing a layer of batting in between the wood and the fabric.

Instant Update

Plush pillows turn posh when layered as a fun focal points.

A few perfectly placed pillows can add an overall cozy effect to your space. Nab an armful of patterned and colorful cushions on sale at a home store, then decorate accordingly: placed on your desk chair, tossed on your bed, stacked on the floor beneath a window. Relax much?

XXX
CRAFT
QUEEN

WHAT YOU'LL NEED
- Wooden headboard
- Tape measure
- Remnant fabric
- Duck Tape
- Staple gun

XX
DIY
101

WHAT YOU'LL NEED

• T-shirt

• Scissors

• Needle and white thread

• Pillow batting (found at a fabric store)

* T-Shirt Pillow Covers

Keep those summertime memories close to your heart (and head) by transforming your camp tees into plush pillows.

WHAT YOU'LL DO

1. Lay the T-shirt on a flat surface and smooth out any wrinkles. Cut off sleeves and cut 2 matching squares (as large as possible) from the body of the shirt.

2. Thread your needle and stitch the right sides (that's sewing speak for side you want showing) together face to face, leaving the last edge half open.

3. Turn the fabric inside out so the right sides face out. Fill your pillow with batting, making sure to get the corners.

4. Handsew the last edge closed and tie off thread.

Quickie Craft Alert!

Set your sights on far-off locales or snag some outfit inspo by hanging postcards or fashion illustrations with mini clothespins on a length of twine. It makes for a fun and inspiring garland, and nixes big, blank walls.

✳ Dreamy Night Light

Artfully drape an assortment of sparkly necklaces and pretty chains around your lampshade to create a pattern on your walls when the sun goes down.

WHAT YOU'LL DO

1. Make sure your lamp is unplugged and on a stable, flat surface.

2. Lightly drape one necklace at a time to create a pattern on your lampshade, overlapping chains as needed.

3. Use the straight pins to secure necklaces in place.

4. Plug in your lamp and turn it on at night to see the shadows cast on the wall.

WHAT YOU'LL NEED

- Lamp and light-colored lampshade
- Assortment of necklaces
- Small straight pins
- Lightbulb

✳ Postcard-Covered Nightstand

Give your bedroom a world-traveler vibe by decoupaging your bedside table with pretty postcards from friends and photos of faraway places. Find them at vintage stores, or online at Etsy or Ebay (everyone will just think you jet set!).

WHAT YOU'LL DO

1. Arrange your postcards and pics in a pattern on the nightstand. Feel free to overlap them for a collage vibe.

2. Use the paintbrush to apply a layer of Mod Podge to the surface of your nightstand.

3. Coat the back of each item with Mod Podge before placing back down, then press in place on the tabletop.

4. Cover the postcards, pics and any part of the tabletop that's still showing with more Mod Podge, using your hands to gently smooth and press down as you go.

5. Scan your work for any air bubbles. Use the paintbrush to paint on more Mod Podge, and use your hands to smooth the bubbles out.

6. Let your project dry for about an hour, or until it feels dry when you touch it.

WHAT YOU'LL NEED

- Nightstand with a smooth top (wood, metal or plastic work!)
- A handful of exotic post-cards and cute pics
- Foam paintbrush
- Mod Podge

✳ Silky Scarf Quilt

XXX
CRAFT
QUEEN

A collection of vintage silk scarves gets transformed into a bohemian coverlet that you can cuddle up with for years to come.

WHAT YOU'LL DO

1. All the scarves should be about the same size in the final quilt, so use the straight pins to tack down the edges of any scarves that are too large.

2. Lay out the scarves in the order you'd like them: one long row makes for a pretty splash of color for the foot of your bed, but we love square-shaped coverlets, too.

3. Ask Mom for help with the sewing machine, and sew the scarves' edges together on the reverse side. The seams will pop up on the inside (aka the reverse side), so the two pieces of fabric will lay smooth on the outside.

4. Once the scarves are sewn together, measure the mattress cover to fit the scarf layer and trim to fit.

5. Measure the linen or cotton fabric to match the mattress cover, and sew edges together using the sewing machine.

6. Use the sewing machine to sew the scarf layer to the backing and batting layer, working with the reverse sides facing each other. Sew three edges together, as well as half of the last edge, then turn the layers inside out so the right sides are facing outside. Handsew the last edge and tie off the thread.

WHAT YOU'LL NEED

- 4 to 6 gently used square vintage silk scarves that are about the same size (try Goodwill)
- Straight pins
- Sewing machine
- An old mattress cover for batting
- Linen or heavier cotton for backing
- Needle and thread
- Scissors

✳ Pretty Drawer Pulls

Decoupaged drawer pulls wake up a sleepy nightstand with a pop of pattern and color.

WHAT YOU'LL DO

1. Remove the current knobs from your nightstand and set them on a flat surface.

2. Cut your fabric into squares at least 3 times the size of your knobs.

3. Apply Mod Podge to the entire surface of the knob, including the base.

4. Wrap fabric around the surface of the knob, smoothing to cover and gathering excess underneath the knob.

5. Use a rubber band to hold the excess fabric in place at the base of the knob. Let dry.

6. Once dry, remove the rubber band and trim fabric excess. Finish with one coat of Mod Podge over the fabric to seal. Let dry overnight, then screw knobs onto nightstand.

WHAT YOU'LL NEED

- Nightstand with wooden screw-on knobs (or buy new, plain knobs at a home supply store)
- Fabric in a fun pattern
- Scissors
- Foam paintbrush
- Mod Podge
- Rubber bands

✳ Pom Pom Pillow Shams

Hello, plush: A few puffs of cheery yarn update your plainest pillows.

WHAT YOU'LL NEED

- Clover-brand Pom Pom maker in largest and second largest sizes (find at a craft store)
- Yarn in colors that match your pillow (try 2 to 3 colors)
- Scissors
- Quilting needle
- Throw pillow

WHAT YOU'LL DO

1. Follow the pom pom maker package instructions and make 10 total from the two sizes. Leave a tail on each pom pom long enough to sew into the pillow (about 10").

2. Thread the quilting needle with the tail of one pom pom, and sew pom pom to one edge of the pillow, being sure to insert the needle up through the pom pom's center and back down into the pillow edge so it's secure. Tie off and trim excess tail.

3. Repeat for four more pom poms along that side, then switch to opposite side of pillow with the five remaining pom poms. Color combos we heart: orange, pink and aqua; green, purple and cyan.

* XOXO Wall Letters

Spell your heart above your headboard for a daily reminder of L-O-V-E.

WHAT YOU'LL DO

1. Make an X and an O template: Use a computer to type a giant X on one page and a giant O on another. You'll need a font size around 650, depending on the type. Print and cut out letters.

2. Lay the foam board on a flat surface. Place letter templates on surface and measure a repeating X, O, X, O so there's enough room on your board. Trace templates with pencil.

3. Remove template, then use T-pins to mark the traced X shape.

4. Repeat step 3, this time with the O template, and then repeat again with the X and the O template to spell XOXO.

5. Tie one end of yarn onto a T-pin and leave a 2" tail. With the other end of the yarn, begin wrapping around each T-pin in the letter to connect all pins with the yarn, crossing and

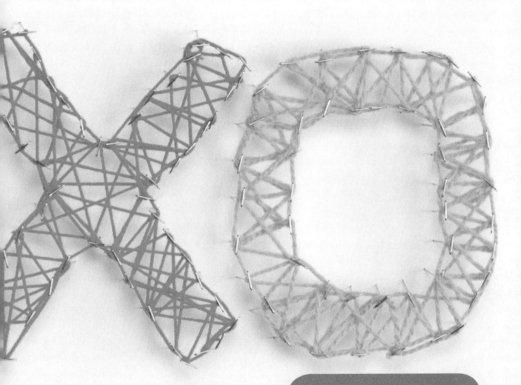

crisscrossing throughout the shape. Tie off the yarn on the last pin and leave a 2" tail. Tuck tails into letter to finish.

6. Repeat step 5 on each letter with a different color yarn. Use mounting squares to hang the foam board on the wall above your bed.

WHAT YOU'LL NEED

- Computer with printer
- Pencil
- Scissors
- Large piece of foam board
- Quilter's pins/T-bar pins (2 to 3 packs of 60)
- Yarn in 3 to 4 colors that match your room
- 3M Mounting Squares

WAKE UP YOUR WALLS & WINDOWS

Energize your room by dolling up your windows and walls. Feels like too big a task? We've got easy ways to make a statement with just a little effort. Try painting a mini mural, tacking up a tapestry or even just a simple snapshot garland. Adding minor details like these can have a major overall effect—especially if they're meaningful to you.

✳ Snapshot Photo Garland

Fun family memories and friend pics are the star in this adorable garland. So festive for the holidays!

XX DIY 101

WHAT YOU'LL DO

1. At home or the photo counter at a drugstore, print your digital pics to 3" x 4".

2. Using a ruler and scissors or the paper cutter, snip a piece of plain cardstock to 3 ¼" x 4 ¼". This will be the first layer under each pic. Repeat so you have 16 layers of plain cardstock (that's one for every photo).

3. Cut a piece of printed cardstock to 4" x 5". This will be the second layer under the photo. Repeat so you have 16 pieces.

4. Draw an X with glue on the back of a photo and center it on the plain cardstock. Use more glue to stick the photo layer to the printed cardstock. Let dry. Cut 17 pieces of ribbon, each 17" long.

5. Punch holes in opposite ends of the printed layer near the top corners. Tie one piece of ribbon to each hole on the first photo card. Use the ribbon in the right hole to connect to the left hole of the second photo card, and so on. You'll have an extra ribbon on each end for hanging on the wall.

WHAT YOU'LL NEED

- 16 photos
- Paper cutter
- Ruler
- 4 types of patterned card-stock
- 2 colors of plain cardstock
- Acid-free glue (safe for photos)
- 5 to 6 spools of ribbon, all 3/8" wide
- Scissors
- Hole punch

Sheer Genius Scarf Curtains

Give your windows a cheap and colorful lift with an easy-breezy window treatment.

WHAT YOU'LL DO

1. Install your curtain rod with a parent's help.

2. Loop about 6" of one scarf around the rod and tie a knot just below the rod, letting the tail fall.

3. Repeat for the remaining scarves, separating them out so there are 3 scarves on either side of your window.

WHAT YOU'LL NEED
- 6 sheer scarves per window (try Target)
- 1 curtain rod per window

Instant Update

TRY IT: Fab floor art

Want to change up your room without ripping out the carpet? Stock up on bright bath mats in a square or circular shapes for a fun take on "tiles." Use them as colorful stepping-stones in your room—and a colorful focal point.

*Glam Scarf Canopy

Who doesn't love the enchanting look of a draped canopy? Get ready for a space that's extra dreamy.

WHAT YOU'LL DO

1. Lightly mark your canopy's center point on the ceiling using a pencil.

2. Hold one scarf 5" from the end and push a T-bar through the fabric and pin to the ceiling. Stretch out the long end of the scarf and pin straight out, but let the scarf drape in the middle just a little bit.

3. Repeat step 2 with the remaining scarves, using the center point as your starting place and working in a circle or star shape.

WHAT YOU'LL NEED

- 5 colorful scarves
- T-bar pins or 3M Mounting Squares
- Pencil

✳ New Paint Job

XXX
CRAFT
QUEEN

A fresh coat of paint can really jumpstart your room's vibe. Pick a palette of two to three main colors for your entire space, then choose one for your wall color.

WHAT YOU'LL DO

1. Use the painter's tape to cover any areas you don't want painted, like wood trim along the baseboard or a door frame or your closet. You might be tempted to skip this step, but don't. It's critical to keep paint off these places—promise.

2. Lay out a plastic drop cloth or an old bedsheet to cover the floor where you'll be painting to protect it from any drips, drops or spills.

3. Open the paint can and stir well with the wooden stirring stick. Pour a bit of paint into the tray and use a brush to create a 1' square patch on the wall. Let your test spot dry for at least two hours to make sure you truly like the shade.

4. Roll the foam roller in the paint tray and begin to coat the wall in paint, moving the roller up and down in a W shape until the area is fully covered.

5. Let dry before repeating with another coat, if necessary.

Instant Update

So. Many. Paint. Colors. Here's how to find the right hue for you.

1. Think about what mood you want your room to have. Sure, your fave color might be hot pink, but a restful green or mellow blue might be worth considering.

2. Head to the paint store and grab 10 paint chips that appeal to you. Once home, check 'em out in different types of light: daylight, lamplight, etc.

3. Tape your top 3 contenders to the wall in your room and sleep on your decision. Still love it? Go buy your paint!

WHAT YOU'LL NEED

- Paint, in your new color
- Painter's tape
- Plastic drop cloth or an old sheet to cover floors
- Stirring sticks
- Painter's tray
- Foam rollers and paintbrushes

✳ Scarf Wall Tapestry

Create a fun focal point with a bright beach cover-up or graphic-print scarf (tassels are a plus!).

WHAT YOU'LL DO

1. Use T-bar pins to tack up each corner of your tapestry to the wall behind or near your bed.

2. Fill in any drooping spots with another T-bar pin as needed.

WHAT YOU'LL NEED
- Scarf, beach sarong or other tapestry
- Quilter's T-bar pins

Quickie Craft Alert!

A room full of fresh flowers is inspiring and relaxing (plus they add a pop of color). Gather a collection of bud vases from around your house or Goodwill, then tie a ribbon bow around the neck of each. Fill each vase with cool water and pop in trimmed stems from the backyard or Mom's garden.

✳ Mini Mural

Love the idea of a mural but don't want to go full scale? This framed version is for you.

WHAT YOU'LL DO

1. Remove the glass and backing from the frame, then hang the frame on your wall with the hammer and nail.

2. Sketch out your mural design on paper before committing to the wall. Use stencils to make a pretty pattern or stamp your initials for a cool monogram or get creative by going freehand with a brush and paint.

WHAT YOU'LL NEED
- Poster frame
- Hammer
- Nail
- Stencil or stamp
- Acrylic paint
- Paintbrush

Free Fixes!

Find a new way to display those photos of you and your friends.

1 ON THE WALL: Pick a unique place, like your ceiling, and use double-sided tape to make a grid of your fave snapshots.

2 AHEAD OF THE GAME: Line your bed's headboard with a row of fun photos. Punch holes in the top of each picture and string them along, or use bitty pushpins or tape.

3 HEARTFELT: Use square photos (Polaroids or print-outs from Instagram) to make a heart shape out of photos and place on the front or back of your bedroom door.

* Chalkboard Anytime Banner

Transform a pennant flag banner into a cheery greeting or positive daily reminder for whenever ya need a pick-me-up.

WHAT YOU'LL DO

1. Remove any stickers from the pennant flags for a clean surface. Squeeze a bit of chalkboard paint onto the foam paintbrush and paint surface of each of the pennant flags.

2. Let paint dry for 24 hours, then paint another coat and let dry.

3. Cure paint by covering entire surface of pennant flag with a layer of chalk, then erase.

4. String pennant flags on a length of yarn, threading through holes. Leave at least 12" on each end to tie onto pushpins.

5. Press pushpins into wall and hang banner, then use the chalk to write a fun message.

WHAT YOU'LL NEED

- 14 wooden pennant flags (find them at Michaels)
- Chalkboard paint
- Foam paintbrush
- Chalk
- Yarn
- Scissors
- Pushpins

Instant Update

Affordable art is all around!

Try web sites like Etsy.com or 20x200.com for cool artwork to fit your babysitting budget. Or buy some frames from a local shop and print out your fave artsy photos. Make a point to take interesting shots next time you travel.

✳ Floating Wall Shelves

A utilitarian wooden crate just needs a quick coat of paint to be transformed into a dimensional (and functional) wall statement.

WHAT YOU'LL DO

1. On a dry, sunny day, lay a few pieces of newspaper in an open space outside. Set a crate on the newspaper and spray-paint the whole surface, coating all sides. Let dry and repeat with a second coat, if necessary. Let dry.

2. Repeat step 1 for all of the remaining crates.

3. Hold a crate horizontally at about eye level on your wall, using a level to make sure it's straight. This one will be at the bottom right. Mark 2 holes, where the nails will fit in between the crate's slats, with the pencil.

4. Use the hammer to bang the nails into the wall, then hang the crate on the two nails, making sure it's flush against the wall and fairly sturdy.

5. Repeat steps 3 and 4 for the remaining crates, hanging the bottom left next and then the top right crate.

6. Fill crates with mementos, books and photos.

WHAT YOU'LL NEED

- 3 wooden crates (try the craft store or your local farmer's market)
- Newspaper
- Spray paint
- Level
- Pencil
- Hammer
- 2" long nails

CUTE UP
YOUR CLOSET

Forget overstuffed sweater drawers and messes of mismatched socks—keeping a neat closet shouldn't be a chore. And with our handy DIYs, it isn't. We'll help you kick clutter, save space and unearth all those cool clothes you forgot you had. It's almost like shopping, but you won't be spending a cent on new threads. Score!

✳ Outfit Inspo Magnets

Mix 'n' match magnets help to solve that age-old dilemma—what to wear?

WHAT YOU'LL DO

1. Flip through old fashion mags and snip out photos of items similar to what's already in your wardrobe, plus any new styles you love or outfits that seriously inspire you.

2. Use photo-mounting squares to attach the magazine cut-outs to the round magnets.

3. Attach a magnetic board to your wall or closet door, and then start creating outfits. So cute.

WHAT YOU'LL NEED

- Magazines
- Scissors
- Round magnets
- Photo-mounting squares
- Magnetic board

Quickie Craft Alert!

Host your BFFs for a fun outfit inspo photo shoot!

Get your girls together for a sleepover photo shoot. Ask each to bring a duffel full of her fave items from her closet, then put them together in stylish combos and start snapping! Post-shoot, print out the images and gift each girl with a mini magnetic board and magnets so she can create her own super-stylish inspo wall.

follow your heart

✳ Candy Jar Corrals

Welcome to the candy shop—accessory candy, that is. Serve up your hair ties, clips, bows and pins in cute glass jars, so you're not scrambling in the a.m.

WHAT YOU'LL DO

1. Rinse out jars and lids and let dry.

2. Remove any stickers from the wooden labels for a clean surface. Squeeze a bit of chalkboard paint onto the foam paintbrush and paint surface of each of the labels.

3. Let paint dry for 24 hours, then paint another coat and let dry.

4. Cure paint by covering entire surface of label with a layer of chalk, then erase.

5. Affix a chalkboard label to the front of each jar, just below the opening, with the hot glue gun. Use the chalk to write the name of the stored item.

6. Fill jars accordingly with hair elastics and bobby pins or whatever accessories you keep handy.

WHAT YOU'LL NEED

- 3 glass candy jars with or without lids (found at a craft store)
- 3 wooden labels (found at a craft store)
- Chalkboard paint
- Foam paintbrush
- Chalk
- Hot glue gun and glue sticks
- Hair elastics, hair clips, bobby pins, bows (we know you own those!)

JANE EYRE

THERING HEIGHTS

SE and SENSIBILITY

✳ Peek-a-Boo Edging Tape

A quick strip of tape adds a bright pop of color to your closet doors. Or get crafty with the door to your bedroom.

WHAT YOU'LL DO

1. Attach the edge of the tape roll to the top of your door's edge. Begin to unroll tape and press against the edge of the door firmly. Watch out for the latch!

2. Use scissors to cut the edge of the tape at the bottom of the door.

3. If the tape is wider than your door's edge, carefully cut the excess tape off the edge of the door with the scissors. Get Mom's help if needed!

WHAT YOU'LL NEED
• Hot pink Duck Tape (or pick your fave color)
• Scissors

Instant Update

6 more easy ways to makeover your bedroom door...

1. STICKER SISTER
Stock up on cute and clever bumper stickers on your travels near and far. Stick 'em on your door, collage-style, so everyone who passes gets a glimpse of your quick wit.

2. QUOTABLE CUTIE
Hang a dry-erase board, then write up a new QOTW (that's Quote of the Week) every Sunday night for powerful weekly inspiration.

3. GREEN GIRL
Use Washi tape to attach a grid of faux flowers on your door. A simple X over each stem should suffice. Welcome to your very own secret garden!

4. PIN-PERFECT
Print out a bunch of all-star pins from your Pinterest boards and make a real-life version on your door. Daily inspo never hurts!

5. MACRAMÉ MAVEN
Ask Mom or Grandma to teach you the awesome art of macramé, or pick up a kit at the craft store and find a how-to online. Then get weaving to create a mini masterpiece that you can hang on your doorknob.

6. POLAROID PRETTY
Print out your fave photos of your besties, family and pets and tape them up in a grid on your door. Change them out every few months for a fresh set of smiles when you grab your threads in the a.m.

✳ Hang-It Handbag Organizer

A vertical organizer highlights those pretty purses to help you switch out your bag. That means Friday's school tote swaps out for Saturday's clutch in a second.

WHAT YOU'LL DO

1. Cut a length of fabric to 32" x 6" to allow for overhang on either side of the foam board.

2. Cut 6 strips of webbing to 7" lengths. Cut 6 strips of the leftover fabric to 1 ½" x 7" lengths.

3. Place a piece of hem tape on the front of a webbing strip, then affix a fabric strip on top, pressing firmly. Repeat for all webbing and fabric strips.

4. Use the needle and thread to sew one side of the 6 snaps onto the webbing strips' backs, about ¼" away from the top.

5. Sew the second half of the snaps onto the opposite side of the webbing strips, so you'll have a loop when the snaps are closed together.

6. Lay out the 6 snap loops flat onto the fabric length vertically so they are about 5" apart. Sew one end of the open loops to the fabric, reverse side facing out. (Hint: Closing the loop will allow the fabric side to show.) Repeat for all loops.

7. Use spray adhesive to affix the 30" length of fabric to the foam board, folding over the excess fabric onto the back. Let dry.

8. Place four Fastener squares to the back of the foam board and attach it to your closet door or the wall.

9. Use the snap loops to hang the handles or straps of your favorite handbags.

WHAT YOU'LL NEED

- Foam board cut to 30" x 4"
- 30" x 36" cotton printed fabric
- Spray adhesive
- 1 ½"-wide nylon webbing
- Peel-and-stick hem tape
- 6 sew-on snaps
- Needle and thread
- Scotch Reclosable Fastener squares

✳ Cinchy Scarf Rings

Every stylish girl knows scarves are a simple way to amp up an outfit. A few shower rings let you flick through your collection in a flash.

WHAT YOU'LL DO

1. Wrap each shower ring with Washi tape, alternating colors and patterns.

2. Attach all of the plastic shower rings from your pack to the bottom bar of the hanger.

3. Hang hanger in your closet, then fill each ring with a scarf. You may need to loop lightweight scarves around the rings so they don't slip out.

WHAT YOU'LL NEED

- A package of round plastic shower rings
- Washi tape in various colors/patterns
- Wooden hanger with a pants bar
- Scarves

Instant Update

Be part of the clean closet club with these three space savers....

VELVET HANGERS: They're ultra-slim, super soft and grippy enough to keep your stuff from slipping.

UNDERBED STORAGE: Don't discount the space beneath your bed—that's precious real estate. Snag a slim storage box for seasonal clothes, and then stash them out of sight.

OVER-DOOR SHOE RACK: Hanging your flips and flats behind your bedroom door means tonsa extra room for that pile of laundry in your closet.

✳ Boho Closet Curtain

A sweeping printed curtain over your closet door transforms a staid space into one that's utterly breezy and a bit bohemian.

WHAT YOU'LL DO

1. Ask Mom or Dad to help you remove your closet doors, if that's an option. If not, simply hang the curtain over top of the door (no one will know the diff).

2. Use a measuring tape to determine the curtain length. Install the hooks or curtain rod above the door frame, so the bottom hem hits where you want it.

3. If using a curtain rod, use shower rings to hang curtain. If using adhesive hooks, hang the curtain from the hooks.

4. Cut a length of ribbon long enough to use as a sash to hold your curtain back on one side. We like it tied in a bow!

WHAT YOU'LL NEED

- Measuring tape
- Adhesive hooks or tension rod
- Shower curtain or window curtain
- Shower curtain rings (if using tension rod)
- Length of ribbon

Instant Update

These three fast fabric updates add texture and color to your space, without any effort.

VELVET PILLOWS: They're ultra-luxe and add a dose of glam to a well-dressed bed or window seat.

SHEEPSKIN RUG: Toss one beneath your desk for a plush footrest while you study, or plunk it in the middle of your floor.

TASSEL TIME: Stringing up tassels on the ends of curtain rods, off doorknobs or on your bedposts lends a lush, free-spirited vibe to your space. Find them at a home decor store.

✳ Frame-It Jewelry Organizer

A simple frame and a few strips of crochet trim are all you need to craft this crafty chic jewelry hanger.

WHAT YOU'LL DO

1. Make sure there's no glass in your frame, then cut strips of the crochet trim to fit the width of the frame.

2. On the wall side of the frame edges, use the picture frame nails to attach strips of crochet trim in rows. One nail on each side should hold it in place. Check your work to make sure the trim is straight.

3. Use one more nail to hang the frame on your wall, then place S-hooks intermittently through the crochet's weave.

4. Use the S-hooks to hang necklaces and bracelets. Place your earring hooks and posts through the crochet weave.

WHAT YOU'LL NEED

- Wood frame
- Crochet trim in different widths
- Scissors
- Small picture frame nails
- Hammer
- Small S-hooks (found at a home improvement store)

Quickie Craft Alert!

Even more cute ways to display your jewelry...

BRANCH OUT: If you want to get extra creative, wrap a few branch twigs in pieces of bright embroidery floss—glue the ends down before hanging.

NAILED IT: Hang up an empty frame, then fill with a cluster of nails and hooks to make an artful jewelry display.

BELT IT: Got a lot of fab jewels? Use a belt or tie organizer to stash your necklaces, wrap bracelets and fave headbands.

GLAM UP YOUR VANITY

Creating a little nook for getting ready will make your mornings a tiny bit more glam and will also nix your daily game of hairbrush hide 'n' seek. We suggest going all-out girly, with a floaty ribbon chandelier, bejeweled hand mirrors and metallic makeup bags. How very pretty.

✳ Vintage Vanity Tray

A dressed-up catchall (with a pop of hot pink) grants you easy access to your fave perfumes, sprays and spritzes.

WHAT YOU'LL DO

1. Trace the opening of the frame or mirror onto the reverse side of the cardstock with a pencil.

2. Cut out the shape in the cardstock, making sure to trim for smooth edges.

3. Insert the cardstock shape into the lip of the frame (psst: you can layer two pieces of cardstock if necessary).

4. Arrange your vanity tray with pretty perfumes and the jewelry you wear every day.

WHAT YOU'LL NEED
- Vintage photo frame or mirror
- Hot pink cardstock
- Pencil
- Scissors

Free Fixes!

Save those bottles...
New ways to upcycle your old fragrances

COLLECT 'EM ALL: Use a pretty, empty bottle to corral your stash of hairties by placing them around the neck.

BUDDING BEAUTY: Set an empty bottle on a shelf with a bit of water and a few blooms.

ALL THE LIGHTS: Stock up on vintage glass perfume bottles and arrange them prettily on your windowsill to catch the sun.

✱ Embellished Hand Mirror

Doll up your looking glass so it's pretty to admire from all angles.

WHAT YOU'LL DO

1. Lay mirror on a flat surface with the back side facing up.

2. Squeeze a thin line of glue around the top corner of the mirror.

3. Place rhinestones along the line of glue, adding more glue and rhinestones to fill in the space of a 2" diagonal section. Let dry.

4. Repeat steps 2 and 3 with a different color of rhinestones until the entire back of the mirror is covered.

WHAT YOU'LL NEED

- Plastic hand mirror
- Craft glue
- Small rhinestones in different colors and sizes

Quickie Craft Alert!

Try this bejeweling technique...

- On the top of your headboard
- On the frame around your door
- On the edges of your bookshelf
- On the case of your laptop or phone

*Jetsetter Makeup Bag

Whether you're toting them to school or on vacay, these customized cosmetic kits will help keep your beauty arsenal organized—and plane friendly (plus they make super cute gifts!).

WHAT YOU'LL NEED

- Clear makeup bag with zipper (found at Walmart)
- A few yards of ribbon in coordinating colors
- Stick-on rhinestones
- Alphabet stickers
- Puff paint or permanent markers
- Tacky glue

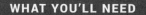

QUICK 'N' EASY

WHAT YOU'LL DO

1. Remove any tags from bag.

2. Use stickers to spell your name across the front. Lay out the ribbon length where you like it, parallel to top of bag. Use a thin line of tacky glue to attach the ribbon to the bag, wrapping all the way around. Ends should slightly overlap in the back. Trim and glue. Repeat if desired.

3. To create a cute pull, tie a short length of ribbon to zipper.

4. Use rhinestones to add sparkle, or doodle with the puff paint or markers.

✱ Lacy Jewelry Catchall

This chic container is as functional as it is fabulous—and the perfect home for your everyday jewelry. It also makes a great gift for your mom or grandma.

WHAT YOU'LL DO

1. Cut a strip of ribbon or fabric long enough to wrap around a tray or dish.

2. Using the foam brush, apply a layer of Mod Podge to the container surface, then position and affix the ribbon or fabric on the container. Smooth out any bubbles. Let dry thoroughly.

3. Apply another coat of Mod Podge over the ribbon, smooth out any gaps and let dry. Trim the edges evenly with scissors.

WHAT YOU'LL NEED

- Lace ribbon or fabric
- Plain white ceramic or porcelain trays/dishes (try Target)
- Mod Podge
- Foam paintbrush
- Scissors

Quickie Craft Alert!

Love decoupage? Here are a few more things to try...

- Paint on a pretty eyelet fabric or trim
- Try a sequined trim for a hint of sparkle
- Use preppy striped ribbon to make one for Dad

DIY 101

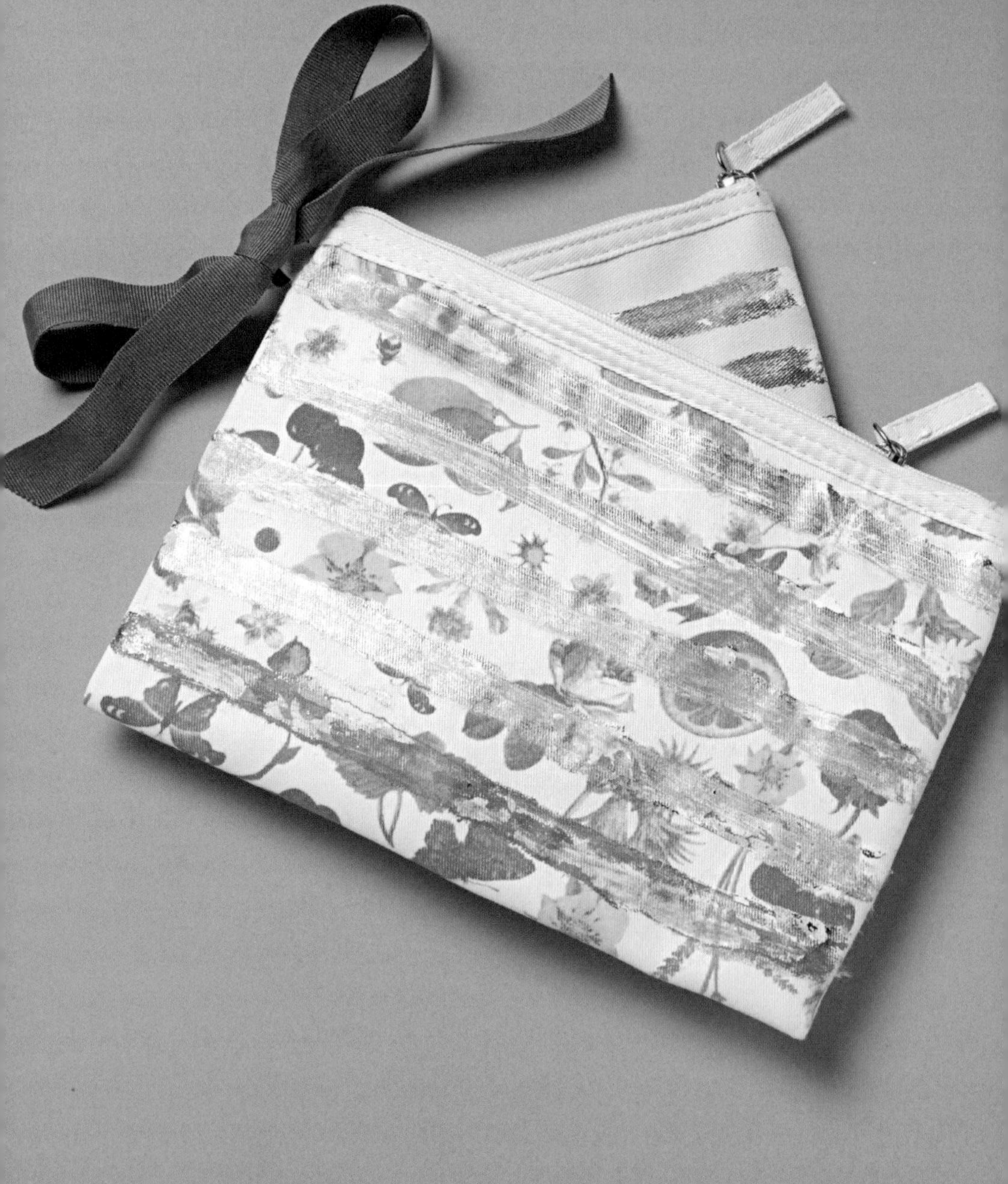

✳ Metallic Makeup Bags

Shiny stripes give a ho-hum cosmetic case plenty of pizzazz. Toss this in your tote for an easy way to find your balm and blush.

WHAT YOU'LL DO

1. Paint a line of transfer adhesive along the base of the cosmetic bag. (It's OK if it's not perfect!) Let dry for 15 minutes.

2. Press a foil sheet with the silver side down on top of the adhesive line. Use the Sharpie (with the cap ON!) to rub the foil sheet onto the glue, pressing hard to make it stick.

3. When you think the foil has transferred (peek under the corner), gently peel off the transfer sheet to reveal a foil stripe.

4. Repeat steps 1 to 3 to make more stripes as desired.

WHAT YOU'LL NEED

- Metallic foil transfer sheets (try the Martha Stewart Crafts line at Michaels)
- Transfer adhesive
- Foam paintbrush
- Sharpie with cap
- Flat canvas cosmetic bag (try Marshalls)

Instant Update

The magic of makeup bags

SWITCH UP YOUR THINKING: A zippered makeup bag can do way more than just hold your lipgloss. Stock up, then try...

CORD WRANGLER: Keeps your earbuds and phone charger exactly where you want them (not in a tangled mess).

TRAVEL KIT: Stash your antibacterial gel, a granola bar and tissues for your next flight or road trip.

HAIR-MERGENCY KIT: Store extra hair ties, bobby pins, mini hairspray and gel for easy access.

✳ Floating Chandelier

DIY 101

Here's the perfect project for all those hair bows and scraps of pretty ribbons you've been collecting: a whimsical mobile that's like a shimmery chandelier.

WHAT YOU'LL DO

1. Cut your scrap ribbons to about 2 feet in length. Fold the lengths of ribbon in half and lay the fold over the side of the hoop, tucking the tails in through the loop that's created to form a loose knot. Pull tight.

2. Repeat step 1 for all ribbons, affixing them around the hoop.

3. Cut the sequin trim to about 18" in length. Fold the trim ends together and loop around the edge of the hoop, pulling tight. Repeat for the rest of the sequin pieces, arranging between ribbons as desired.

4. Screw the small hook into the ceiling above where you want your mobile to hang. Cut 3 pieces of monofilament—each around an arm's length—to measure how far the mobile will be suspended.

5. Tie each monofilament to the hoop so they form a triangle shape, then gather the strings at the top in one hand and tie together. Place this knot over the hook to hang your mobile.

WHAT YOU'LL NEED

- 8" embroidery hoop
- 26 yards of ribbon in various colors
- Scissors
- Small screw-in hook
- 3 yards of sequin trim
- Monofilament string (found at a craft store)

Quickie Craft Alert!

Make your chandelier unique with these special touches.

GO BOHO: Tie on colorful floaty feathers of all shapes and sizes

GO EARTHY: String up wooden beads and shells

GO PREPPY: Bright grosgrain ribbons in bold colors will show your stripes

✳ Makeup Brush Mason Jars

xx DIY 101

Monogrammed mason jars are perfect to stash makeup brushes and eyeliner pencils on your vanity. They also make sweet gifts for Mom or a friend.

WHAT YOU'LL DO

1. Apply a bit of craft paint to the foam paintbrush, then paint the bottom of the jar so it looks like it was dipped in paint. The dip-line edge should be smooth, but not necessarily straight.

2. Clean your brush with water and repeat step 1 for the second jar, using the other paint color.

3. Let paint dry, then using the second foam brush, smooth on a coat with of Mod Podge to seal the paint.

4. Let Mod Podge dry, then attach the initial stickers to the front of each jar to monogram. Use a hot glue gun if necessary.

WHAT YOU'LL NEED
- 2 Mason jars
- 2 foam paintbrushes
- 2 colors of acrylic paint
- Mod Podge
- Plastic initial stickers

Instant Update

Fresh flowers for a fresh look

A leafy plant or a trio of freshly picked blooms does wonders for sprucing up your space. Whether you buy a bouquet at the store or snip a few daisies from the backyard, just taking the time to bring nature inside can give you a whole new outlook on your room. No green thumb? Fill a bud vase with faux flowers instead.

EVERYTHING
ELSE

From photos to flowers to candles, it's the tiny touches that make your room a reflection of Y-O-U. Fill your shelves with teeny terrariums, honor your favorite childhood picture books and line your desk with tissue paper flowers. Now's the time to show off your true style.

WHAT YOU'LL NEED

- 2 yards satiny fabric per ball
- Martha Stewart Circle Cutter
- 6" Styrofoam ball (find in the floral section of your craft store)
- Hot glue gun and glue sticks
- 12" ribbon for hanging

✳ Bouncy Fabric Pomanders

These fuzzy fabric balls are sure to brighten any space: hang them off your curtain rod, on your door handle or off the posts of your bed. The options? Endless.

WHAT YOU'LL DO

1. Use the circle cutter to cut 3" circles out of all your fabric.

2. On one circle, add a drop of hot glue in the center.

3. Fold the circle in half, then add another drop of hot glue at the middle of the fold and carefully fold the right side of the half circle up and into the middle.

4. Place another drop of hot glue onto the bottom of the triangle side, then fold the left side of the half circle over top. You should now have a triangle shape.

5. Repeat steps 2 to 4 for all circles.

6. Use the tip of your hot glue gun to make a small indent in the Styrofoam ball. Repeat this step, making a straight line of indents all around the ball, then add a few drops of glue to one of the indents and insert the point of the fabric triangle. Hold fabric straight for a few seconds to allow glue to dry.

7. Fill all indents with fabric triangles, then make another line of indents and continue until the ball is filled with fabric petals. Note: It's helpful to section off the ball in quadrants so you don't squeeze the fabric triangles in too tightly.

8. Loop the ribbon in half and hot glue the ends down at a point on the ball. This will be your hanger.

Instant Update

Shake up those drapes! Fun twists on window style

Sometimes all you need is a new perspective. The curtains that frame your windows should be fun, not frumpy. Change out drab drapes for ones in a totally crazy color, like bold orange. Or, try swapping the finials on the ends of your curtain rod for something DIY-ed. Don't hold back! Make new tie-backs out of funky plaid shirts or Dad's old ties.

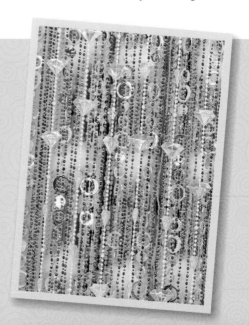

✳ Glitter Magnet Dots

Pop these sparklers on a metallic surface or magnetic board for some shiny happiness.

WHAT YOU'LL DO

1. Separate the magnets and lay them on the cookie sheet so they won't slide around as you work.

2. Paint the tops of the magnets with glue, being extra careful not to let the glue drip down the sides.

3. Sprinkle glitter over magnets, covering the surface.

4. Let dry, then stick them wherever you please.

WHAT YOU'LL NEED

- 3/4" round magnets (found at a craft store)
- Craft glue
- Small foam paintbrush
- Loose glitter in different colors
- Aluminum cookie sheet

✳ Washi Tape Photo Frame

Drop in a pic of your besties, then place this pretty frame prominently.

WHAT YOU'LL DO

1. Plan out the pattern you'd like to create with the Washi tape (we used 3 different prints to make this design).

2. Apply tape to the corner of the frame and use scissors to carefully trim ends to fit. Press down across length of tape to seal.

3. Continue to apply tape in your chosen pattern to the frame surface, being careful to snip edges and keep lines straight.

4. Add a fun photo to the finished frame.

WHAT YOU'LL NEED

• 4" x 6" photo frame with wide border

• Washi tape in varying colors and widths

• Scissors

• 4" x 6" photo

QUICK 'N' EASY

✳ Teeny Terrariums

Terrariums add a gorgeous living element to your room, are simple to make and easy to keep alive— even if you weren't born with a green thumb.

WHAT YOU'LL NEED

- Polished rocks
- Small open glass container
- Tiny stones or shell gravel
- Potting soil
- Small succulents and indoor plants, like ferns or ivy
- Preserved moss (try Home Depot)
- Miniature creatures, like faux butterflies and bugs (try Michaels)
- Spray bottle with water

WHAT YOU'LL DO

1. Lay polished stones in the bottom of a clean, dry glass container—this helps with drainage. Pour a layer of gravel on top, making the combined stone layer about 1" thick.

2. Scoop some potting soil into your container on the top of the stone layer. Lightly mist soil with the spray bottle until damp.

3. Gently remove the plants from the packaging, being sure to handle the roots lightly. Work with the largest plant first. Dig a small hole in the soil layer and bury the roots (get help dividing the plant if the root ball is too big). Add more soil if necessary. Repeat for remaining plants. Make sure not to overcrowd—the plants shouldn't touch the glass walls.

4. Lay out your landscape: Fill in open areas with damp moss, stones and miniature creatures. Thoroughly mist with water.

WHAT YOU'LL NEED

- 6 sheets of colored tissue paper
- Twist tie or flexible metal wire
- Scissors
- Ruler

✳ Blooming Tissue Paper Flowers

These ethereal tissue paper poms add a pop of color and chicness to your space.

WHAT YOU'LL DO

1. Stack tissue paper together so edges meet. Measure an 8" x 4" rectangle and cut it out through all layers.

2. Begin to accordion fold along the short side of the tissue paper stack, creasing folds at ½" wide. Repeat for the full length of the tissue paper.

3. Use a twist tie or cut a 6" piece of wire, then wrap around the middle of the stack of folds and twist to secure, leaving the wire ends long.

4. Trim the corners of the square ends of the tissue paper so they form triangular points.

5. Gently separate the layers of tissue on one side of the wire, fluffing out each layer to make a round shape. Repeat on the other side.

Instant Update

4 fab paper flower uses

GARDEN PARTY: Wrap flowers around your bed posts for a nature-like feel.

PENCIL TOPPER: Create a fun reason to do your homework by using the twist tie to top off a pink pencil with a big bloom. Add glue to secure.

WINDOW INSPO: Hang flowers from strips of ribbon on your curtain rod for an unexpected art installation.

CROWNED PRINCESS: Fashion a flower crown using seven to eight blooms and a plastic headband.

✻ Braided Rug

Stock up on remnant fabric from the craft store, then spend your TV time braiding. Soon, you'll have a cozy rug to call your own.

WHAT YOU'LL DO

1. Lay out your scrap fabric and make 2" cuts every 2" along the width. Then, tear the cuts so the fabric rips down the length of the piece, leaving you with a bunch of 2" wide, long strips. (The length will vary depending on the fabric.)

2. Repeat step 1 for all pieces of scrap fabric.

3. Begin to braid by choosing 3 strips of fabric and tying the ends together, leaving a 1" tail. Braid the strips to the end of the length (if one is shorter than the others, tie on another piece of fabric and attempt to camouflage the knot within the braid). Tie off the braid once finished, leaving a 1" tail.

4. Repeat until you have about 40 to 48 braids.

5. Lay the canvas cloth on a flat surface. Line up your braids in the order you prefer, then stick each one down to the canvas by applying fabric glue directly to the canvas and pressing the braid on top, in a straight line. Add the next braid in the row and so on, using more glue as you go.

6. Once all braids are laid down on the canvas, let glue dry overnight.

7. Then, thread your needle with yarn and sew along the edge of the canvas to tack down each individual braid—you're sewing a line just before the braid's knot on each end.

8. Untie the knots and trim the fabric ends to make a uniform length of fringe trim.

WHAT YOU'LL NEED

- 12 to 15 yards of scrap fabric (each piece should be around 30" long)
- Scissors
- Heavy-duty canvas cloth cut to 2' x 2.5'
- Fabric glue
- Yarn
- Quilter's needle

✳ Twinkling Teacup Candles

Glow on with this charming candle inside a dainty cup.

WHAT YOU'LL DO

1. Ask Mom for help melting the wax in a double boiler until the temperature hits 180 degrees.

2. Meanwhile, use a bit of the wick adhesive to secure the wick to the bottom center of a clean, dry teacup.

3. If you're using a scent, let the wax cool to 125 degrees, then add 3 to 4 drops of desired fragrance. Stir well and pour the wax to the very top of a prepared teacup.

4. After 15 minutes (or until wax is almost set), sprinkle surface with glitter. Let the wax finish setting. Trim wick to 1/4" before burning.

WHAT YOU'LL NEED
- Double boiler
- Soy candle wax and wick adhesive from Michaels
- 3" wicks (Michaels)
- Pretty vintage teacups (try Goodwill)
- Thermometer
- Fragrance or essential oil (optional)
- Large old metal spoon
- Gold loose glitter
- Scissors

✳ Picture Box

Create a cute case displaying your hobbies or trinkets from trips far and wide: It's like a 3D scrapbook—no funky glasses necessary.

WHAT YOU'LL DO

1. Prop your materials (such as ribbons, pictures, other trinkets, etc.) in the box so that they'll stay in place when your box is standing upright.

2. Once your placement is planned, use glue or pushpins to keep all the items secure.

3. Close the back of the shadow box or frame and place in a spot where you can admire your work.

WHAT YOU'LL NEED
- Shadow box or deep frame
- Materials that reflect your hobbies or travels
- Glue
- Pushpins

XX DIY 101

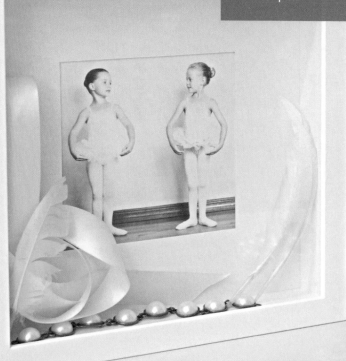

✳ Lookbook Art

You don't have to spend tons of money to fill your room with cool pieces. Highlight your fave childhood reads in a fun gallery.

QUICK 'N' EASY

WHAT YOU'LL DO

1. Carefully remove the cover or favorite illustrated pages from beloved picture books.

2. Crop the pictures so they fit within your frame.

3. Remove the frame backing and place the page inside the frame, then replace the backing.

4. Hang your frames on the wall or prop up on a shelf.

WHAT YOU'LL NEED

- Favorite childhood picture books (or scour yard sales for copies of your faves)

- Scissors

- Picture frames in a variety of sizes

✳ Envelope Photo Holder

Cheery envelopes hide favorite photos so you can mix up and switch out to your heart's content.

WHAT YOU'LL DO

1. Choose two envelopes and glue the flap of the first envelope to the bottom of the back of the second envelope.

2. Repeat step 1 until you have used the remaining envelopes.

3. Mount the envelope chain on the wall with pushpins.

4. Slide your photos into the pockets of the envelopes, letting them peek out at an angle.

WHAT YOU'LL NEED

• 10 bright envelopes

• Glue

• Pushpins

• Printed photos

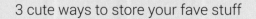

Instant Update

3 cute ways to store your fave stuff

STUFFED ANIMALS: Borrow a basket from Mom and coat with white spray paint. Stow furry friends in a chic new spot.

BANGLES AND BRACELETS: Want a fun new way to lasso your arm candy? Try old flour and sugar canisters, a small pegboard with pushpins or a belt hanger.

YOUR MAGAZINES: Those piles of issues you've read a zillion times but can't throw away yet? Sturdily stack 'em up in a little tower on the floor and top with a small tray for a fashionable side table.

CHAPTER TEN

MAKE IT YOURS

From bringing in personal touches to keeping your space clean (it's actually easy!), here's how to make your mark.

LAYER IT

The most beautiful bedrooms look like they've been well loved, lived-in and layered over time. There's no reason why your first pointe shoes can't hang next to your fourth grade horse show ribbon or your little tikes soccer trophy—they all make up who you are.

In fact, it's those smaller items—artwork, trophies and mini mementos—that add the finishing touch to a gorgeous room. Get creative in the way you display your favorite things and be proud of them as a part of your history.

Preserving the past

Here are 3 ways to showcase your meaningful objects:

1. Create an ode to a treasured hobby, like in our Picture Box craft on page 120.

2. Hang small tokens, like BFF bracelets or handmade necklaces, off the Clipboard Pin Wall (page 29).

3. Set up the Floating Wall Shelves on page 72 and fill with your collection of trophies or awards.

CLEAN UP YOUR ACT

Now that you have a well-organized, clutter-free and totally cute new room, you've already taken several steps in making it that much easier to keep clean, tidy and looking good while you're showing it off to friends and family.

Plus, don't you feel less stressed when your bed is made, your laundry is folded and there aren't shoes littering the floor? Knowing everything has a place and is in that place can be very calming. Making an effort to keeping a neat room isn't as hard as it seems. In fact, you can make a major dent in as little as five minutes.

Cleaning routines
Here's what to do when you only have...

5 MINUTES: Toss all clothes, clean or dirty, that are on the floor into your laundry basket for sorting at a later time (just don't forget!). Pull the covers up on your bed and open the curtains. Tidy up any other surfaces (especially your desk) if possible.

15 MINUTES: Pick up any clean clothes and put them out of sight to be folded later. Behind a pillow usually works! Toss dirty clothes in the laundry basket. Make your bed. Open the curtains and blinds and empty the trash. Organize the surface of your desk into piles.

30 MINUTES: Pick up and put away any clean clothes or shoes on the floor. Make your bed and fluff the pillows. Open the curtains and blinds. Take out the trash and recycling. Straighten any loose papers on your desk, shelve any scattered books and give all visible surfaces a run-through with a clean feather duster.

1 HOUR: Pick up, fold and put away any clothes on the floor. Make your bed and fluff the pillows, straighten the duvet. Open the curtains and blinds and crack the window if possible. File any stray papers on your desk and take out the trash and recycling. Tuck away any cords or chargers. Put away jewelry and shelve your books. Run the vacuum quickly and give all your surfaces a quick dusting with a polish cloth. Make sure each area of your room is mess-free and looking tidy.

SWEET SCENTS

We're not going to lie: the first thing that many people notice when they walk into a house is the scent that greets them at the door (chocolate chip cookies baking? Good. Cat litter stink? Not so good.). So make sure your room's scent leaves a positive impression on anyone who enters—but most importantly, on you.

The key thing to remember is to start with a fresh, clean canvas. Masking odors is a lot more difficult than just getting rid of those foul smells in the first place.

A few tips on keeping your room fresh: Always open your windows at least 15 minutes before any friends arrive to let in a nice breeze. Have a designated area for dirty laundry where any smelly socks won't offend you—or anyone else. Fresh flowers on your desk, dresser or nightstand are always a good idea, and you might want to invest in a small bottle of room spray in a favorite scent to top things off. After all, aromatherapy (like a fresh spritz of rosewater, mint or lavender) can have powerful effects on lightening moods and calming minds.

HOME AWAY FROM HOME

Whether you're traveling to Grandma's house for a weekend, bunking up at camp for a few weeks or simply spending the night at a friend's house, creating a sense of home and comfort wherever you go is important. It can mean the difference between enjoying your time away or feeling anxious and unable to doze off.

The easiest way to do that? Bring a couple small reminders from your room to help you feel happy wherever you lay your head. A small photo, your Bible, a favorite stuffed animal and maybe even a tiny spritz of room spray can work wonders. Pack your comfiest slippers, robe and a small pillow or blanket so you have some things of your own to curl up in. When it's time to turn out the lights, you'll hardly be able to tell you're not in your own bed.

SLEEPOVER CENTRAL

And when it's your turn to invite friends to spend the night, go the extra mile to make their stay especially super comfy. As the hostess, be sure to have plenty of pillows and blankets in case guests get cold or feel uncomfortable. Plug in a small night light and make sure each girl has lots of room to stretch out and sleep comfortably. Fresh towels and even a spare toothbrush or slippers will prove your hosting prowess. Your room (and your attitude!) should feel warm and welcoming. After all, your brand-new, totally cute, creative and inspiring room is your happy place, and it should make others feel happy, too.

ALL STYLING AND CRAFTS BY JESSICA D'ARGENIO WALLER
SPECIAL THANKS TO DORMIFY, DORMIFY.COM.

COVER • PHOTOGRAPHED BY SEAN SCHEIDT

CRAFT AND ROOM PHOTOGRAPHY
STEVE BUCHANAN • 42, 44-45, 47, 60, 62-63, 66, 69, 80, 120-121
ERIK KVALSVIK • 38, 41, 43, 56, 61, 65, 108, 123
VINCE LUPO • 74, 83
BRION MCCARTHY • 22-23, 30, 58-59, 98-99, 100, 110-114, 118-119
SEAN SCHEIDT • 20, 24-29, 31-32, 34-37, 48, 51-55, 70-73, 77-79, 84, 87-88, 90, 93-95, 103-104, 117, 128
DAN WHIPPS • 96-97